A Bird and His Worm

Written and illustrated by James Kaczman

Houghton Mifflin Company
Boston 2002

www.houghtonmifflinbooks.com

The text of this book is set in 16-point Caecilia Bold.
The illustrations are ink and watercolor.

Library of Congress Cataloging-in-Publication Data
Kaczman, James.
A bird and his worm / James Kaczman.
p. cm.
Summary: A bird who doesn't like to flap his wings and the
worm he has befriended learn the dangers of trusting strangers
as they travel south together for the winter.
ISBN 0-618-09460-1
[1. Birds—Fiction. 2. Worms—Fiction. 3. Travel—Fiction.
4. Strangers—Fiction. 5. Safety—Fiction.] I. Title.
PZ7.K11646 Bi 2007   [E]—dc21   2002000216

Printed in Singapore
TWP   10   9   8   7   6   5   4   3   2   1

For my wife, Libby

There once was a bird who did not fly. He preferred to walk. All the other birds thought his behavior was very odd, so he spent most of his time by himself.

"Why don't you fly?" asked the other birds.

"I don't really have anything against flying," explained the bird, "but I love walking around and seeing all the beautiful flowers, the interesting plants, the fascinating insects . . . and besides, I don't like to flap my wings."

"He is very odd," the other birds said to one another as they flew away.

One day, while the bird was searching for seeds, he came upon a worm who had just poked his head out of a hole in the ground.

"Please don't eat me!" shrieked the terrified worm.

"I wouldn't dream of eating you," replied the bird. "Unlike other birds, I eat only seeds and berries. You are slimy and squishy. I find you completely unappetizing."

"Thank goodness!" gasped the worm.

"Since it's such a beautiful day, perhaps you would like to join me for a walk?" asked the bird.

"I think that is a splendid idea," answered the worm.

So they strolled along together and chatted happily for the rest of the day.

The bird and the worm went on many long walks together and quickly became close friends.

"I'm glad you don't fly," said the worm.

"So am I," replied the bird.

But soon, winter approached and the bird realized he would have to go south to a warmer climate.

The other birds had already begun their long flight.

"What are we going to do?" the worm asked the bird worriedly.

"We are clever fellows. We will find another way," answered the bird.

The bird and the worm decided to set out walking the long journey south. Along the way they met a fox going in the same direction.

"We are traveling south for the winter," the bird explained to the fox.

"It's a long journey. Would you mind giving us a ride for part of it?" asked the worm.

"Why, certainly," answered the fox slyly. "You can ride along on my back."

The bird and the worm climbed up on the back of the fox.

"Now this is the way to travel," said the bird.

"We are so clever," added the worm.

They are not so clever, the fox thought to himself. *When I get hungry I will just turn my head and gobble down the bird and—why not?—the worm as well.*

The bird and the worm chatted with the fox as they traveled along. At first, the fox could think of nothing but eating up the bird and the worm in one big gulp.

But he soon found himself enjoying his conversation with them. He lost track of time, and several hours had passed before he began to realize he had grown enormously hungry.

Suddenly, the fox swung his head around! His sharp white teeth flashed as he opened his jaws wide and . . .

...he stopped.

"I can't eat you," he told them. "Now that I have gotten to know you as the charming, funny fellows you are, it is impossible for me to devour you in one big gulp as I had planned."

"Now I have to return home to my den," the fox
went on. "But I must tell you, you are not clever at all.
You were just lucky this time. I think you would be
foolish to get a ride from a fox again."

"That is very wise advice," said the bird.

"Thank you," added the worm. "It was a pleasure
meeting you."

A bit further on, the bird and the worm came upon a snake traveling in the same direction. "Would you mind giving us a ride?" asked the bird. "We are tired and we are not supposed to get a ride from any foxes, but you are clearly not a fox."

"I will be happy to give you a ride," hissed the snake. The bird and the worm hopped onto the snake's back.

The snake thought to himself, *What a delicious meal these little fools will make.*

The snake was hungry, so he decided to gobble down the bird and the worm right away. He quickly whipped his head around! His sharp white fangs flashed as he opened his mouth as wide as he could and . . .

"Wait! Stop!" shouted the bird. "You can't eat us! We are charming, funny fellows!"

"Once you get to know us you will be unable to devour us!" added the worm.

"I don't want to get to know you," hissed the snake. "I find you tiresome and annoying."

He snapped his jaws shut, but the bird and the worm jumped out of the way just in time and fled.

They ran into the bushes and hid from the snake.

"He is not very nice at all!" exclaimed the bird.

"It's a shame he never took the time to get to know us," lamented the worm.

The bird and the worm remained hidden in the bushes until the snake slithered off. Then they continued on their journey.

"I don't think we will be asking anyone else for a ride," said the worm.

"Certainly not," answered the bird. "We are clever fellows. We will find another way."

The bird and the worm walked to a nearby airport
and flew the rest of the way south in an airplane.

"I don't really have anything against flying," said the
bird. "I just don't like to flap my wings."